For Mom, Dad, and Sgt. Rock

Thanks to Scott Cunningham, Kate Farrell, and Melanie Comer for their editorial prowess and patience.

Thanks also to Calvin Pyle, Chris O'Connell, David Saylor and Janna Morishima, Jonathan O'Connor, Tommy Collins, James Farrell, Peter Kuper, Russell Christian, John Meyer, Cheung Tai, Leyah Jensen, Sandy Jimenez, David Whitmer, and Jill and John Wodnick.

Henry Holt and Company, LLC
Publishers since 1866
175 Fifth Avenue
New York, New York 10010
www.henryholtchildrensbooks.com

Henry Holt® is a registered trademark of Henry Holt and Company, LLC.
Copyright © 2007 by Kevin C. Pyle
All rights reserved.
Distributed in Canada by H. B. Fenn and Company Ltd.

Library of Congress Cataloging-in-Publication Data
Pyle, Kevin C.
Blindspot / by Kevin C. Pyle.—1st ed.
p.   cm.
ISBN-13: 978-0-8050-7998-2
ISBN-10: 0-8050-7998-X
1. Graphic novels. I. Title.
PN6727.P96   B65 2007   2006041155

First Edition—2007
Printed in China on acid-free paper. ∞

1 3 5 7 9 10 8 6 4 2

BLINDSPOT

by kevin c. pyle

HENRY HOLT AND COMPANY • NEW YORK

before...

en I heard we were moving
ain I don't remember being
rticularly upset.

The only thing I really liked about our
house was the oddly placed linen
cupboard right above my bed.

would lie in bed at night
and imagine that all the
things of my dreams were
n there, waiting for me
to fall asleep so they
could come out and play.

MATH PROBLEMS

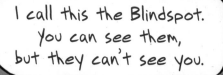
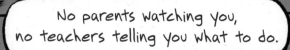

RECON

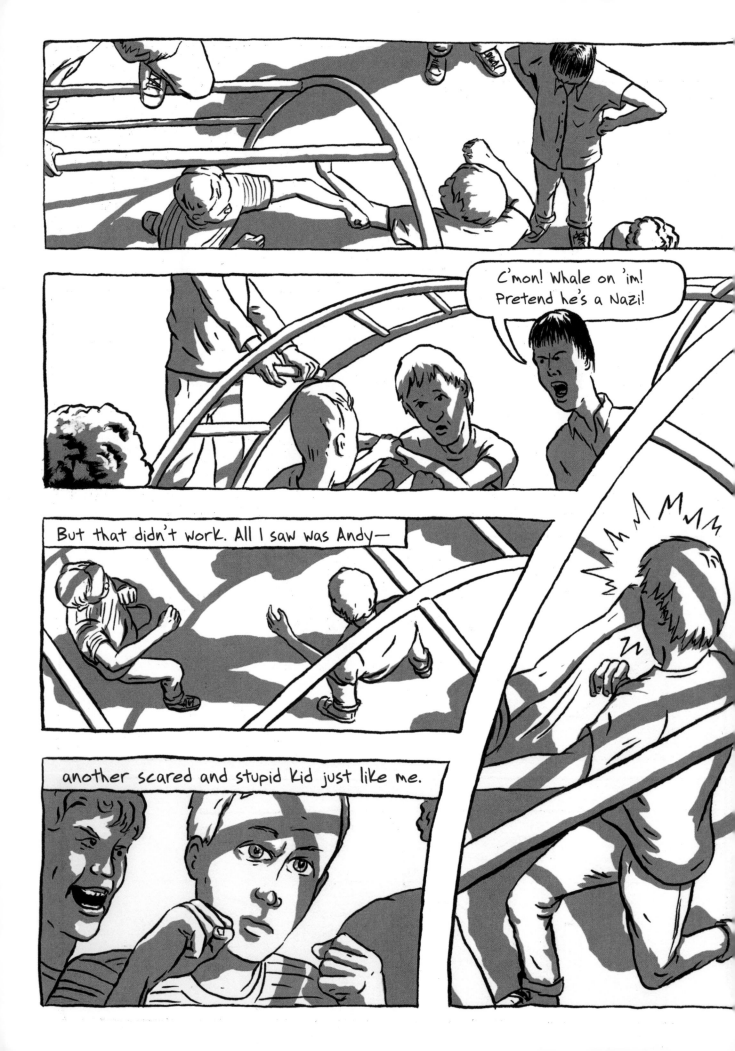

SCRUNCH

LET'S GO!

I'll keep watch.

Whatever.

WOW!

What is THAT called?

INTERROGATION

Dean, Dr. Goldstein will see you now.

THE FIRST RULE OF INTERROGATION IS TO PLAY DUMB...

HAVE A SEAT, PLEASE.

IF YOU DON'T KNOW ANYTHING, YOU GOT NOTHING TO SAY.

I HAVE SOME SIMPLE WORD TESTS I WANT YOU TO TAKE.

THOUGH I WAS STARTING TO KNOW SOME THINGS.

NOW, THERE ARE NO RIGHT OR WRONG ANSWERS ON THESE TESTS...

THINGS I WISHED I DIDN'T KNOW.

...AND YOU WON'T BE GRADED ON THEM.

BUT I WASN'T ABOUT TO LET HIM KNOW THAT.

OKAY, NOW LET'S GET STARTED.

BLINDSPOT

SCRUNCH
SCRUNCH
SCRUNCH

I just kept thinking that if
I didn't move or say anything...
he might forget that I was there.

But he just kept talking.

...well, I got out of
there in one piece...

sort of.

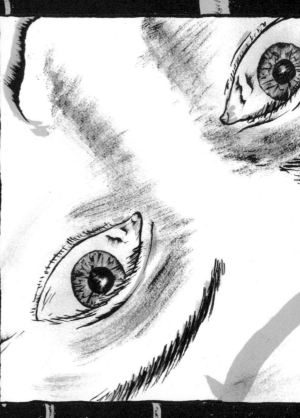

After a while it was like I didn't even hear him
anymore. I just looked up at the stars.

Then it
came to me.

How they might be eyes.

The eyes of God that have seen all the things that have happened to all the people in the world.

Then I thought how they never move—they just hang there and don't do anything but blink.

Then I thought again of all the things they've seen—all the bad things.

And how those eyes
don't save anyone.

That the only one who can save you
is another person. Or yourself.

But you have to know someone's in
trouble before you can save them.

You have to have the eyes of God...
but the heart of a real person.

R & R

SPRING

FWOOP!

after

Sept. 2001